Rose in Bloom

Sharon E. Cathcart

Rose in Bloom

JUNE

Mis Mehefin

"You've always wanted to write; this is the perfect opportunity."

My Aunt Susan, who always says that if life gives you lemons you should make limoncello, was doing her best to cheer me up about my recent layoff.

"They gave you an excellent package; you won't have to look for work for a year. My friend has a cottage in a town about 90 minutes outside of London that you can have rent-free for six months. There's even a fellow who comes over to do the caretaking and gardening, and he'll continue to be paid. It would be doing both of you a favor while she stays with her daughter in Scotland."

Aunt Susan's friend, Katherine Tremaine, was a college sorority sister whose daughter had just had a baby and was not doing well. Postpartum complications had set in and Katherine needed someone to live in Wisteria Cottage from late July until just after the new year turned. She would send a key to me if that would suit, and I could leave it in the house when I left; she had an extra.

I had spent much of my life waffling when daring opportunities presented themselves, and most of the time I said no. I prided myself on my practicality. Sensible business suits, sensible shoes, sensible angle bob hairstyle … always practical. Even my fingernails had a sensible French manicure.

It was a legacy of my parents, always reminding me to be sensible or practical when I wanted to do something out of the ordinary. Like just about any child, I wanted to make my parents happy.

Where had that gotten me, at the end of the day? Nowhere. I lived 500 miles from my parents, who were retired. My dad, who had been practical his entire life and saved to enjoy retirement, was now experiencing health problems with no firm diagnosis as yet. He'd never stepped outside his life plan.

The lesson was staring me right in the face: not all plans work out, and sometimes you should do something impractical.

The timing couldn't be better; the lease on my apartment was ending and there was nothing stopping me. So, I had everything packed up and put into storage except my clothes and my laptop, and bought a ticket to London with an open return date and made arrangements for transportation to a little village in the Downs. If it turned out be miserable, I'd come home early and stay in a hotel while I looked for new digs. Katherine Tremaine and Aunt Susan would just have to understand. Maybe the caretaker, whom I imagined as a smiling grey-haired fellow, could live in.

What I didn't expect was how I fell immediately in love with the little ashlar brick house covered in the wisteria vines that gave it its name. Two chimneys, mullioned windows, split door, cozy furniture in shades of blue and green, fireplace, books and games in the cupboard. There was no television, but I could stream things on the laptop if I felt like it and the wi-fi cooperated. Honestly? I didn't miss it.

The garden was obviously planned, but gave the impression of a natural wildness. The flowers, in shades of red and purple, were stunning. Trees gave off a good amount of shade, and there was a table and bench for when I felt like eating outdoors, or just sitting and watching the stars.

The house also came with an orange tabby cat, Marmalade, who delighted in following me everywhere, including into the garden, and sitting in a nearby chair whenever I was working. I had a lovely view from the window over my desk, and I found the words from my manuscript flowed readily in a way they hadn't at home.

The train ran with reasonable regularity from Berwyn to Paddington Station, so I could go into London whenever I wanted; I had only to call a ride share or taxi to get there. The nearest village to me, Shalbourne, was a little less than a mile away, and I walked there almost every day to pick up groceries at the market and my mail from the post office inside it. I was in better shape than I'd been for most of my life.

Aunt Susan was right, of course; I needed the break from all of the pressure I'd put on myself. The words came easily on the novel I'd always wanted to write. I soon donated several of my sensible suits and shoes to a local charity shop. While I mostly opted for jeans and t-shirts, I still fixed my hair and wore makeup; I wasn't ready to give that up. You never knew who you might meet, after all; there was no excuse for not keeping up appearances.

I am pretty sure that was also something my mother had drilled into my head along the way.

JULY

Mis Gorfennaf

I'd been at Wisteria Cottage for about two weeks when the gardener showed up for the first time. I was a little worried when I saw him; Gareth Llewellyn had dark hair in a thick braid nearly to his waist, a bushy beard, and generally looked disreputable in corduroy pants, a baggy shirt, battered fedora, and green Wellingtons. He reminded me of the homeless men I saw on the streets back home, except that he smelled good. He was accompanied by a delightful little blonde boy who introduced himself as Timothy Rhys Edwards, informed me that he was seven years old and had the same middle name as his uncle, and then introduced his Cocker spaniel, Flash. I reminded myself that looks could be deceiving; Llewellyn's manners were impeccable, and he did the weeding and trimming with alacrity while the dog and boy played on the back lawn.

"I'll see you next time," Timothy called out as they put their tools in the car. "I get to see my uncle Gareth most weekends in the summertime."

After settling the boy in the vehicle, Llewellyn walked back to the door to talk to me.

"I'm sorry, Miss Davis. He's my sister's boy, and can be a little enthusiastic at times. He lost his father last year, so I try to see him regularly. If he's too much for you, just say. Mrs. Tremaine told me that you're a writer, and I'm sure you need your peace to do that.

"On the contrary, Mr. Llewellyn; please bring him with you. He made me smile. And please, call me Rose."

A smile through the beard. "Thank you, Rose. Call me Gareth."

I watched them drive away, Timothy waving enthusiastically from the rear window until they were out of sight.

The week passed quickly; I sent letters to friends since the internet at the cottage was unreliable, and I sat out in the garden reading or writing whenever the weather was nice enough to do so. I had to admit that Gareth's work made for a delightful place to spend my time.

One day, I realized that the migraines that had plagued me for years seemed to have disappeared. They were so debilitating that I had injectable medication to stop them, and now I didn't need anything stronger than a Beecham's powder from the chemist in town. I hoped that I wouldn't need those very often.

I also noticed the tension leaving my shoulders. At last, I admitted to myself that the job that deemed me redundant had made my life miserable. My constant drive to prove myself to managers who most likely couldn't pick me out of a police line-up was for naught when the layoffs came, and now here I was.

I'd left the top of the front door open, and the kitchen door at the rear to get a cross-breeze in the house. I heard the Range Rover pull up in front of the cottage, and the rattle of garden implements being taken out.

"Hello the house," Gareth called.

"I'm coming," I said, and hurried to unlatch the front door. "You can come through here."

"I'll just go 'round to the gate rather than track anything in on those nice rugs. Just wanted to let you know I was here."

Timothy and Flash followed.

"May I show you my new game, Miss Rose? Uncle Gareth says I'm meant to ask permission before just starting, since you might be busy with your book."

"That would be wonderful."

Soon I was engaged in a pattern matching game on Timothy's iPad, which proved harder than one might imagine if the shapes didn't line up. Timothy was gracious in winning and in loss, and before long it was noon.

"You and your uncle must stay for lunch," I said. "It's nothing fancy, just cold cut sandwiches and crisps. But I would like your company. Why don't you go ask him?"

Timothy came back to say yes, and his uncle followed, wiping his Wellingtons on the back porch mat before entering. Soon, we were sitting around the kitchen table, chatting about the garden and eating our meal. Timothy seemed to do most of the talking.

"I like coming here with Uncle Gareth. I like it when I get to go on his jobs. He has another one in the city, but it's not time for me to go to that one yet." He seemed to have wound down.

"Don't wear out Miss Rose with things she needn't worry over," Gareth said. "I thank you for the lunch, but I need to finish up. Things take a little longer without my helper." He winked at his nephew and then went back out the door.

Timothy and I went back to the sitting room, where I dealt cards for a hand of Go Fish.

"Your uncle is very fond of you," I said.

"He's a good person. My mum says she doesn't know what she'd have done without him since my Da died. But Mum says she wishes Uncle Gareth wouldn't go about looking like a wild man from the Fen, whatever that means. She says he decided not to cut his hair until he has a forever lady, and that's been a while. She doesn't think he's trying very hard, either." He sighed. "Do you have any threes?"

"Well, maybe if he cut off that big beard so a lady could see his face, it would help," I replied as I handed over the cards. "He's a very nice man, though he doesn't talk much. I'm sure he'd look more handsome without it."

"Do you have a gentleman friend back home in America, Miss Rose?"

"Timothy, that's enough."

I wondered how long Gareth had been standing behind us.

"It's time to go; come help me load up the tools. Good day, Rose. I'll be here the same time next week."

Aunt Susan called that evening to find out how things were going, and I told her about my progress on the book. I also mentioned Gareth and Timothy.

"And what do you think of Mister Gareth Llewellyn? Katherine tells me he's rather dishy."

It was a good thing we weren't on Zoom; that way, no one could see my eyes rolling.

Dishy? Was she crazy?

"Aunt Susan, I am only going to be here for six months. I don't think of him in any way at all, except as the gardener. A very capable one, to be sure; the garden is stunning. But he's fairly unkempt. I definitely do not find long hair and big beards attractive."

"You never know when you'll find a diamond in the rough, dear. When did you become so doctrinaire?"

"Aunt Susan, I'm just being practical." The penny dropped. "Are you and Mrs. Tremaine up to something?"

"Whatever makes you say … oh, dear! The timer's going off on my baking! Toodle-oo!" She hung up the phone.

My aunt Susan didn't bake. In fact, she said she was the only person alive who could burn water. The kitchen was not her bailiwick.

One of the things I'd loved most about Aunt Susan when I was a kid was how lively and colorful she was. Her blonde hair was long and curly, her make-up and jewelry were bold, and she wore bright, flowing clothes.

I wanted to be just like her. I loved the kind of costume jewelry that my mother, Julia, called "gaudy." I made scarves into skirts that I wore over my little jeans and t-shirts until Mom took them away when I was about six years old.

"You need to be practical, Rose," she'd said, tucking a lock of her brown, bobbed hair behind one ear. She wore pearl button earrings, a plain gold wedding band, a polo shirt and khaki pants. It was pretty much her uniform.

"You're six years old," she continued. "You need to stop playing pretend. You need to get serious. My sister is no role model. Your father and I have discussed the matter, and there will be no arguments."

I didn't understand why my mother was so upset, but I wanted to make her happy. So, I pushed the things that made me smile to the back of my mental closet.

I hadn't thought about that day in years, but the memory was vivid. From then on, I'd ticked all of the practical boxes … right down to choosing the most appropriate boyfriends. Men with good jobs, who wore suits to the office and had stock options. Men with names like Trent, Brad, and, in one particularly godawful instance, Clint.

I liked the GQ types, certainly; men who were well-groomed and as at home in a tuxedo as they were in their casual Friday chinos. But it never felt right; I wasn't a priority to them unless they wanted a hostess … and after a while they all felt soulless.

If I were going to find Mr. Right, he would have to meet an exacting set of standards that I couldn't articulate — not even to myself.

I had indeed become doctrinaire — just like Julia — when all I'd wanted was to be like Susan. I'd wanted a life full of color and light; instead, I'd taken on a life devoid thereof. It gave me pause.

Unlike my aunt, however, I could cook.

"Uncle Gareth, Miss Rose sure is nice." Timothy was playing on his iPad in the back seat of the Rover.

"Mmm. That she is." Gareth kept his eyes on the road back to Berwyn, but his mind was on what Katherine Tremaine had told him about Rose Davis before she'd moved into Wisteria Cottage: a successful business woman who, if her aunt Susan was to be believed, hid her depression under a facade of hard-edged perfection and control. A woman who felt that polish and practicality were the answer to all problems. He'd presumed she'd be dour, possibly even matronly, with a pinched mouth.

I couldn't have been more off-base if I tried.

"And she's pretty. I like her red hair."

"I think, technically, it's auburn."

Dark, rich auburn. That looks like silk. I'd love to run my fingers through it.

"Well, it's pretty." A short pause. "Uncle Gareth, maybe you should do what she said and cut off your beard. I know you heard what Miss Rose said."

"It's my beard, and my decision."

Gareth thought about what he'd overheard. It was true that his sister was after him to give up the ridiculous vow he'd made … which, to be honest, had never included letting his beard grow out for as long as he had. Maybe it was time for the beard to go.

Or at least time to think about it.

When Gareth dropped Timothy off, he went inside to see his sister for a few minutes.

"I'm thinking of shaving off my beard," he announced.

"Hello to you, too! As to the beard, you'll have no complaint from me," Bronwen replied. "I can't help wondering, though; Timothy has nattered on for the past week about nothing so much as the pretty red-haired American lady staying at Wisteria Cottage. Might she have anything to do with it?

Gareth's cheeks heated up under the beard; he was glad Bronwen couldn't see him blush. He cast his eyes down to the floor before muttering "Maybe."

"Are you going to ask her out, Uncle Gareth?"

"Remember what Mrs. Tremaine said, Timothy. Rose is writing a book. She's a very busy person."

"She has to eat some time," Bronwen put in. "But I suspect she'd rather not do it whilst sitting across from a wild man from the Fen."

When I walked into Shalbourne to buy groceries, I noticed the nail salon. I hadn't had an actual manicure since arriving and decided to indulge myself. Instead of my usual French manicure, I asked for a sparkling coral shade. Baby steps.

I also saw a short-sleeved sweater in the window of one of the shops — jumper, I needed to remember — in a similar tone to the nail enamel and bought it. My hands were shaking as I paid for the garment. I had no idea when I'd wear it, but it would be there waiting when the time was right.

On Saturday morning, I stood in front of the armoire and wanted to scream. So many practical, permanent press blouses ("they'll wear like iron," the saleswoman had promised, and I'd bought several in white and ivory) and so few fun things. I needed to do something about that, sooner rather than later. I dug out a pair of jeans, some sandals, and the new sweater. I felt comfortable and liked how I looked, but my stomach was in knots. Even this small step outside my comfort zone was difficult, but I was determined to do it. I pretended to myself that I wasn't dolling up for company.

When Gareth and Timothy arrived that afternoon, Gareth had done the most ridiculous thing I'd ever seen: he'd braided his beard down to a point, so that he had plaits both at the front and back of his head. I rolled my eyes as I watched the two of them go into the garden and get to work.

To each his own.

I was deep in my writing when, about an hour later, Timothy came in and asked if I'd go outside. "Uncle Gareth wants your help with something."

I followed the boy out to where Gareth sat at my outdoor table.

"Timothy tells me you think I should cut off my beard." He stripped off his leather work gloves and dropped them on the table.

My cheeks heated up; I knew my face was red. "I spoke out of turn. I'm sorry."

"Well, I wondered if you would do the honors of starting the process." He handed me a pair of scissors from a leather shaving kit on the table. "We can put the clippings in with the weeds; I promise to clean up. Just cut off the braid; I'll do the rest."

He tilted his chin up at me and waited.

It was an oddly intimate thing to do for a man I'd only seen three times. I had to straddle Gareth's lap to get close enough; he put his hands on my waist to steady me. Firm, strong hands.

Drawing a deep breath, I took hold of the braid and cut it off close to his chin. I was sure I was red all the way to my hairline; I'd never looked into his deep, hazel-brown eyes before. They were gorgeous, flecked with green, and his gaze didn't waver.

I tossed the braid onto the pile of garden clippings that would be wrapped up and taken away when the gardening was done.

"Thank you, Rose. I'll take it from here." He produced a mirror, a beard trimmer, and a battery-operated razor from the bag.

I nodded and went back inside. I tried to focus on my writing again, but was distracted by what I'd just experienced. It was entirely new, and I couldn't quite process it. I felt like I'd seen Gareth Rhys Llewellyn's soul.

I was sure that most of what I wrote that afternoon would be garbage, but that's what editing was for. I was determined to stay out of the back garden. I couldn't decide if the day was warm, or it was just me. I made typo after typo.

After only a few minutes, I couldn't stand it anymore. I went into the kitchen and got lemonade out of the icebox, along with three glasses from the cupboard, and took it outside on a tray.

Gareth had his back to me, his shirt draped over the chair where he'd been sitting. He was lean and muscular and, when he heard me put the tray down on the table, turned to face me as he finished running the beard trimmer over his chest. The vaguest dark shadow remained across his pecs. He brushed the stubble away, bent over the pile of weed trimmings.

Oh, God. Oh, God. Dimples to die for, and built like a brick house. And those lips.

Stop it, Rose. This is not sensible.

Gareth hurried to put on his shirt. "I'm sorry; I didn't expect you to come back out so quickly."

I tried to look everywhere but at him. "I thought a cold drink would be nice for all of us."

"Is something wrong?"

"No … no."

"Why aren't you looking at me? Surely I'm not that hard on the eyes. Maybe I should have kept the beard to hide my Quasimodo mug?"

"My mum says he's downright handsome when he tries," Timothy announced as he and Flash came bounding up to the table.

I finally managed to raise my eyes to Gareth's as I put the tray down. "He most certainly is."

I didn't want to be sensible anymore. In fact, I wanted to throw caution to the wind.

Dishy didn't even begin to describe Gareth Llewellyn.

I wanted to kiss him. Dear God, how I wanted to kiss him.

Gareth looked into Rose's blue eyes. Until she cut off his beard, he'd never noticed that their pale color was ringed in a darker shade.

He felt naked without the beard, and couldn't say what had prompted him to cut off his chest hair on top of it. He buttoned his shirt, conscious of how the fabric felt against his newly-bared skin.

A literal clean breast of it, perhaps. I wonder how her hands would feel ...

Stop it, Gareth.

I poured the lemonade, a little surprised that I didn't spill any. My hands trembled, which was utterly ridiculous.

He was just the gardener, for crying out loud … and I'd be gone in, what was it now, five months? Dimples … and a gorgeous mouth … and six-pack abs … shouldn't make me so weak in the knees.

"I'll fix us some sandwiches," I said, trying to break the tension.

"Do you need help," Gareth asked.

"No, you finish up out here; I'll bring the lunch when it's ready." The idea of being in close quarters with him was more than I was ready to handle.

I came back outside with a stack of sandwiches and a more calm demeanor. We sat down to eat, and things seemed normal again.

Gareth asked about my book, and I talked about the romance novel I was writing … and the lay-off that had put me in a position to take this time away to live in Wisteria Cottage while I worked on it. I felt as though I were talking with a dear old friend, and the questions he asked when he found out I was writing a romance were intelligent and far from the condescension I'd come to expect from dates who called my hobby "Mommy porn."

Then he said he liked my jumper.

That night, I called Aunt Susan. I talked about Gareth again … and how attractive I found him without the horrible beard.

"Maybe you should indulge in a little affair while you're there, Rosie. It couldn't hurt."

"Maybe … but what if it does? He's smart, and polite, and we talked about so many things this afternoon. What if it hurts because I'm leaving at the end of it all?"

"Worry about that later, dear. Sometimes, you need to live for today."

"I was thinking that very thing."

After we got off the phone, I went to the mud room and found a laundry basket. I took it upstairs to the bedroom and opened the armoire doors. Every business suit and practical no-iron blouse went into that basket; I would decide what to do with them later. For now, the basket was shoved into the corner. I studied the few remaining items; the basic tees and jeans, sneakers — trainers — and practical shoes.

I needed a new wardrobe, there was no doubt about it. And I'd be damned if it would be filled with ivory, camel, beige … or anything labeled permanent press. I didn't want to be that person anymore.

I felt a weight lift from my shoulders the moment I arrived at that decision.

I pretended that it had nothing to do with Gareth Rhys Llewellyn.

"Gary! You shaved!"

"Bronny, your powers of observation are unparalleled."

"He shaved his chest, too," Timothy announced as he and Flash ran through the living room.

"Did you indeed?"

"I see your magazines, Bronny; women seem to prefer their men less … furry … nowadays. And I just cut the hair shorter there. Manscaping, I think you all call it?"

"Mmm. I see." Bronwen turned her attention to her son. "Timothy, stop running in the house!"

Gareth couldn't stop thinking of the expression on Rose's face when she'd come outside with the lemon squash. She'd recovered well, but he hadn't imagined how her eyes softened and her lips moved just before she spoke.

Or how he'd wanted to taste those lips.

It had been a long time since he'd felt that drawn to a woman.

Too long.

Of course, she was leaving in a few months. Still, as Bronwen pointed out, she had to eat some time. When a good opportunity presented itself, maybe he'd invite her to the local for a pint and a bite to eat.

I made a list of things I needed and got the train into London for a shopping trip. I also had my hair cut; I didn't want that angled bob anymore. A soft fringe curved around my forehead and face, and there was texture at the ends. I came home with my arms full of packages and a joyful heart. I put away all of the colorful new things I'd bought and tried to decide which things I'd wear on Saturday. I had a rather lovely summer dress in turquoise blue, and sandals to match.

The next weekend, it poured rain. So much for the dress and sandals.

I looked out the window, somewhat miserable despite my new sage green top and jeans. I didn't expect to see Gareth, but there he was, in waxed jacket and Wellies, ready to do what he could in the yard. Timothy and Flash were not with him this time; he explained that his sister had decided to keep the boy at home rather than cope with a muddy mess.

I had a pot of chicken soup going on the stove; I'd picked up the ingredients the day before in the village, where the grocer had told me it was going to rain and I should be ready. Practical advice, of course. My cooking was a point of pride, so I gathered up the necessary items. I could hardly believe I'd walked home so comfortably with groceries in the folding cart I'd found in the mud room; before coming to England it sometimes took all I had to walk a few blocks! I'd relied so much on the car; it was almost embarrassing.

After a particularly hard cloudburst, I heard thunder … which meant I'd missed the lightning. Gareth let himself into the mudroom, soaked to the skin despite his waxed jacket.

"Gareth! You're drenched. You can't stay in those wet things."

"I can't track mud through the house, either. Katherine let me keep a change of clothes here, just in case. They're in the guest room armoire; nothing fancy, just something clean to drive home in. If you could bring them to me …"

And then I noticed his teeth chattering. Even a summer rain could chill a person to the bone.

"I'm coming back with a robe; take your things off and I'll run them through the laundry while you take a hot shower."

I found his change of clothing, jeans, trainers, and a zip-front hoodie, and brought my white terry cloth robe to the mud room. Ever practical, of course.

"You know where the bathroom is, obviously. We'll have soup when you come down."

If Gareth felt silly in my robe, he didn't show it as he walked by.

"I put my clothes in the washer and started it; the Wellies are on the back porch to be rinsed later." He went upstairs and I heard the water running in the clawfoot bathtub, then the jingle of the shower curtain rings as he pulled them along the rail.

I tried not to imagine what he looked like in the shower.

I failed.

I'd had a fire laid in the grate since I came to the cottage, figuring that I wouldn't need it before fall. It was certainly chilly enough to warrant a fire, so I set a match to the newspaper at the bottom of the stack of logs and kindling. Luckily, it caught quickly and warmed the room. Marmalade took up a spot on the chintz print chair.

When Gareth came back down, his hair was loose over his shirt, damp black tendrils curling at the ends.

"I apologize for my appearance; I didn't know where you kept your hair dryer and I could do only so much with a towel."

"You can always sit in front of the fire …"

"My hair goes rather curly if I just let it dry or don't braid it; you should see it when it's short."

"If you cut it short at the back and sides, and left it longer at the top, I think it would be gorgeous." I clapped my hand over my mouth. It really was none of my business.

"I made a promise to myself not to cut my hair until I had what Timothy calls a forever lady, but I'll bear that in mind. The braid keeps it out of the way when I'm working; it's practical."

"I see."

I glossed over the whole "it's practical" thing; I didn't care if I never heard the word again.

I was far more hung up on "forever lady." And how I would be leaving.

Rose, those thoughts are entirely premature. Stop it. Live for today.

"Help me move that table over by the fire," he said, indicating the game table in the corner of the room. "We can eat here and both be warm."

After we rearranged the furniture, I went out to the kitchen to bring the soup in.

Over lunch, Gareth told me about his other job, teaching music ("I sometimes conduct an orchestra, but mainly I teach"). He had a home in London and came down to take care of the cottage for Mrs. Tremaine, a long-time family friend. It gave him a chance to visit his sister and her little boy, which proved helpful since losing his brother-in-law to cancer.

"Timothy is quite a lad," he said. "He's resilient as can be, and I'm glad to spend time with him. But he needs a role model, and Bronwen, my sister, needs a bit of a break at times. It's not been easy for her, obviously."

After lunch, Gareth insisted on helping me do the dishes. He washed and I dried, and put everything away. We moved the game table back to its appointed corner. I put his clothes into the dryer.

Gareth looked out the window over my desk. "It's still pissing down, excuse my language."

"It'll be a while before your things are dry; you may as well get comfortable."

He sat down on one corner of the blue tufted couch. "Sit with me, Rose."

I sat down next to him, conscious of the heat from the fire and in my cheeks. He draped one arm across the back of the couch, just above my shoulders.

"Thank you for lunch. It was delicious. And I don't think I told you yet how well that color suits you. Or that I like your new hairstyle."

"Mmm." How is it that I was at a loss for words all of a sudden? I latched on to the easy part of Gareth's compliments. "I like to cook, and it's always more fun when there's company."

"Rose. Look at me."

I turned my face toward him, and he leaned in for a kiss. He cupped my cheek gently with one hand and pressed his lips to mine.

If I'd been standing, I'd have lifted one foot from the floor and pointed my toe; that's how good that first kiss was. I opened my lips and let him slide his tongue past my teeth. I entwined my fingers in that still-damp, raven-dark mane.

Gareth's strong hands slid down my shoulders and to my waist, and then under my shirt, touching my bare back. I didn't want to stop.

Gareth pulled away first.

"I've wanted to do that since I first laid eyes on you," he said. "And I love the way your fingers feel in my hair."

I twisted a lock around two of my fingers; when I slid them out, the black ringlet I'd made remained, elongating as the weight pulled it down.

"I told you …" he sighed, as I made another ringlet, and then another. We moved to a large ottoman in front of the fire, where his hair dried into a mass of waves

"I would love," I whispered into his ear, "to see your hair spilling over your bare shoulders."

It was the work of a minute to unzip the hoodie, which he dropped on the floor. He pulled a few locks forward on each side and stood up. "Like this?"

God, he should model for my book's cover. Those jeans fit like a glove, and ...

"Exactly like that."

I reached out a tentative hand and touched his pecs, where the cropped black hair made a shadow. His response was to lift my hand to his lips and kiss the palm. Then he took me in his arms for another kiss.

"Your hands feel so good on me." His voice was barely above a whisper.

"It's still pissing down outside," I said. "Would you like to stay for dinner?"

"What shall we do until then?" His breath was warm against my ear as his lips brushed across my jaw.

"I have a few ideas …"

"We could go upstairs …"

"Or stay right here in front of the fire. There are some quilts and featherbeds in that closet between the book cases."

I'd always fantasized about making love in front of a roaring fire, but never dreamed it would happen on an English summer day, rain beating on the tile roof. Gareth took his time, using his hands and tongue to bring me to a fever pitch before finally entering me. His black hair was a curtain around us as we kissed, caressed, and gave ourselves to one another.

Afterwards, when we'd dressed, we bundled up in one of quilts and fell asleep together on the couch. I felt safe and cosseted in his arms.

When we awoke a couple of hours later, Gareth braided his hair and folded up the clothes that were now warm from the dryer. The rain had stopped.

"I need to go home, Rose. I have to feed my dog."

"If you want, you could come back … and bring the dog with you."

Gareth took a deep breath. "Or, you could come with me. You'll want an overnight bag, though; it's a bit of a drive to come back here from London tonight. I can drive you back tomorrow, or put you on the train."

I had my bag packed in less than five minutes. I filled Marmalade's bowl with dry food and locked the door behind us.

Gareth hoped he wasn't talking too much once they were on the road to London. He told Rose about the house he'd bought there ("something of a crumbling ruin") and patiently restored over the years, one room at a time.

"My grandfather, back in Wales, taught me a lot about fixing and building, and I am glad of it. My place is big enough for Bronwen and Timothy to visit and have us all be comfortable, but not so enormous that we get lost. It puts me close to work and shops."

"I am sure it's beautiful," Rose replied. Her smile warmed his soul.

He reached over and took her hand, letting it go only to shift gears, the rest of the way into town. He pointed out the sights, like the Cherhill White Horse, and promised to show her around Stonehenge, Bath, and Salisbury when their schedules permitted.

I feel like a schoolboy, giddy with my first crush.

I don't what I expected Gareth's house to look like, but I had definitely not imagined a three-story masonry townhouse with a detached garage in the back. Gareth insisted on carrying my overnight bag inside after he put away the garden tools.

"I thought I'd put you in the green bedroom," he said as I trailed behind him. "You could have the blue one if you'd prefer."

The moment we entered the house, we were interrupted by a very enthusiastic black Lab.

"No, that will be fine." I petted the dog, who was introduced to me as Bella.

I was speechless as Gareth showed me the ultra-modern kitchen (which featured a cream enameled compact Aga stove that I immediately wanted to cook on), dining room, and parlor, with a grand piano, downstairs, a cozy living room in shades of grey and tan, with a picture window, and the master bedroom/bath on the next floor. The two guest rooms were on the floor above. It was on the third floor landing that I met Meezie, the Siamese cat ("Timothy named her; he's the one who found her").

Gareth sat my bag on a bench at the foot of the bed while I took in my surroundings. The bedroom walls were a gentle, pale green that reflected the carpets on the hardwood floors. The comforter was patterned in green and gold, and the bed was so high that there was a step stool.

"Your home is beautiful," I managed. "Your hard work has certainly paid off."

"Thank you. The only place I love more is Wisteria Cottage; Mrs. Tremaine has been a family friend for as long as I can remember. She and my mother were at school together."

"That's how she knows my aunt Susan, too. My aunt did a study abroad program." I didn't confess how badly I had wanted to do the same; I had, of course, been dissuaded by my mother since it wasn't practical. I worried that we were falling into banality.

Another deep breath from Gareth. "I didn't want to presume, and I'll understand if you want to stay in the guest room. But honestly, I'd like it if you stayed in my room tonight. I'd love to wake up with you, Rose."

"Then," I said, picking up my weekender, "we should take my things downstairs."

Gareth's room, at which I'd barely glanced on the way upstairs, had dark paneling and floors, with red Turkish carpets that coordinated with the duvet. The attached bath, in shades of creme and brown, had steps up to a sunken jet tub more than large enough for two and a separate shower.

"You did all this yourself?"

"I had contractors for the electrical and water, but everything else I did by myself or with help from Tim, my brother-in-law, before he got sick. Sometimes I think this house saved my sanity."

"It is beautiful."

This time, it didn't feel banal; it felt important to acknowledge the hard work Gareth had put in.

"It is made more beautiful for having you in it. Make love with me again, Rose." He held out his hand to me. "Please."

I put my hand in his and followed him to the bed. Soon we were under the covers and Gareth worked his magic again. His kisses set me on fire as he moved from my mouth down to the most sensitive of places, using his tongue with tremendous skill and gentleness to take me to the peak of excitement before entering me at last. He whispered my name over and over as we moved together.

He was the most exquisite lover I'd ever had. More concerned with my pleasure than his own, he left me thoroughly sated.

Afterward, we availed ourselves of the tub; I twisted my hair up with a clip to keep it out of the water.

"You look very pretty with your hair like that," Gareth said as I stepped into the roiling, warm water.

I thanked him for the compliment and leaned my head back against the edge of the tub. Again, I felt stress leaving my body and being replaced with a serenity that was both new and completely natural. I realized that what I felt was a sense of belonging rather than merely fitting in. I hoped it would last.

When we got out of the tub and got dressed again, I offered to make dinner. We went down to the kitchen and I rummaged through the fridge. There were a lot of ready-made items that only needed heating, and it occurred to me that Gareth was seldom cooking for more than one. I pulled out a couple of packages of microwave chicken biryani and vowed to myself that I'd cook a proper meal for Gareth one day soon. I said as much, since it seemed a shame to waste an amazing kitchen.

"I thought I'd need a kitchen like this," he replied, "but it seems the only thing I ever use is the kettle and the popty-ping. Please, if you feel like cooking, order anything you like from the food halls or Tesco and have it delivered. The numbers are on the fridge."

"I'll make a plan for next time, then."

"I shall look forward to it."

After our meal, Gareth asked if I'd like to hear him play. I had certainly not expected to see a concert grand piano in the house, so I accepted eagerly.

"What would you like to hear?"

"I don't know, surprise me." I sat down on the bench next to him.

The first piece was a set of variations on "Away in a Manger" that he was working on for the Shalbourne village fete, which included a delightful jazzy section. Then, he segued without hesitation into a Chopin polonaise, and finally to an Elton John song for which he also sang.

I was, for lack of a better way to put it, blown away.

"I had no idea you were so talented," I said.

"Madame, you have cut me to the quick!" His smile assured me that the was teasing. "Piano lessons since the age of four, and a long tradition of Welsh singing brought me to this place."

"Do you play any other instruments?"

"Several, since I teach orchestra, but the piano and guitar are the main two, so that I can sing."

Gareth slid an arm around Rose and drew her closer.

"What about you, Rosie. Do you play any instruments?"

"Not a one." She shook her head sadly. "Lessons weren't practical."

"Let me give you one, then. This is middle C." He took her hand and placed it gently on the keyboard, then showed her how to make a chord. "Everything starts from here."

Then he taught her "Heart and Soul" so that they could play together. He couldn't remember the last time he'd smiled so much.

After the song was done, Gareth took Rose in his arms again. "Shall we go upstairs and make a different kind of music together?"

Rose's eager kiss was all the answer he needed.

AUGUST

Mis Awst

I arranged for a charity shop to pick up the clothes I'd put in the basket. I didn't even want them in the house anymore. They belonged to a person I no longer cared to know. I had learned things about myself that I'd never realized before. The old Rose Davis used practicality and perfection to try to control her life … and to hide the fact that she was a depressed, miserable mess. If no one could see that, it couldn't be true.

When I shed my depressed, miserable life and sent its trappings packing, I discovered a different person inside myself. That person, unlike the old Rose Davis, was very much attracted to a long-haired musician who was also good at gardening and building things. There. I'd admitted it.

That weekend, Gareth went up on a ladder to clean the Wisteria Cottage gutters. Timothy and I sat downstairs, playing Snap.

"Tell me about this forever lady business," I said.

"It's something my Da explained before he died. He said Mum was his forever lady. Your forever lady or gentleman is the person you want to spend the rest of your life with. You know, to be together with forever. You'd do anything to make that person happy, even small things, and you can't imagine being with anyone else. He said some ladies like gentlemen and some like ladies, and the same with men … and that it's okay either way. That's all."

"Your father was a very wise man."

"Would you like to see his picture?" Timothy picked up his ever-present iPad and showed a photo of a lovely blonde woman ("That's my mum; she's fair like Granny and Uncle Gareth is dark like Papa") and a brown-haired man with blue eyes. "That's before he got sick, of course."

He put down the tablet after looking at the photo for another moment. "Do you have a forever person, Miss Rose? You didn't answer me when I asked before."

"I don't, but I would like to have a forever gentleman one day."

"Snap!" Timothy cried, and took my cards.

"Why did your uncle decide to stop cutting his hair until he had a forever lady?"

"He thought he had one once. I was just a real little kid when he met Megan. She was from Wales, too, and she sang. She was pretty, but she wasn't nice. I don't know if you know about Meezie, my uncle's cat? Well, we found her in the snow at the Christmas market. She was scared and cold. I put her in my coat and we tried to find where she came from, but no one had lost a kitten. Uncle Gareth said he'd take her home, but Megan said to leave her there because it was bad enough having a dog in the house. Megan didn't like pets. Even though Bella and Flash came from the dogs' home, because they didn't have people anymore. She didn't understand." He looked up at me, eyes shining with moisture. "We all knew that Meezie would have died if we left her there in the snow. She was just a baby. Uncle Gareth said that was the last straw and that when they got home Megan should pack her things and go elsewhere."

"Oh, dear."

"Well, it turned out that she had another boyfriend anyway; Mum says Megan was using Uncle Gareth to get ahead, whatever that means. Anyway, Uncle Gareth thought Megan was his forever lady, but she wasn't. He got real sad and stopped looking after himself. I mean, he ate and bathed and things; he wasn't completely gone, Mum said. He only had the beard for like a year, but he hasn't had a haircut since before Megan left. Mum says he had something called depression, and it was only working on the house in town, and Mrs. Tremaine's house here that kept him going."

Neither of us had looked at the cards in a while.

"Do you like my uncle, Miss Rose?"

I could only nod and look away from the earnest little face shining up at me. There seemed no point in getting anyone's hopes up when I'd be gone in a matter of months. Still, Gareth's way of dealing with depression was not so different from my own; we'd created suits of armor after our own fashion.

SEPTEMBER

Mis Medi

The days were cooler by the time I typed "the end" on my manuscript. Gareth's gardening attire now included a heavy grey-brown sweater that he told me was made of wool from black Welsh sheep. It was early autumn, and the garden needed to be prepared for winter.

We drank mugs of steaming tea with our sandwiches at lunch time now, and Gareth laid a fire in the grate before he went to work outdoors. There was a shed full of seasoned wood that he said I'd be glad of.

"These walls are thick and keep in the heat pretty well once the place is warmed up … but you need to get it there first."

Timothy came bursting in through the back door, Flash hot on his heels.

"Wipe your feet, young man," Gareth called. "And Flash's."

"Yes, sir." The sound of feet scraping the mat, and then the swish of a towel I kept for the dog. Then, Timothy ran into the kitchen. "Miss Rose, my whole form at school is meant to go to the

Natural History Museum in London. My mum is a teacher in another room, and she said we need more chaperones. That's a big word for grown-up helpers. Uncle Gareth is meeting us all at the train station. Will you come, too?"

"Well, I'd have to meet your mother first, and make sure I'd be welcome."

"I'm sure you would," Gareth said. "But yes, you should meet Bronwen."

So, it was arranged that I would join Gareth and Timothy at Bronwen's home for supper next Saturday after the gardening was done.

I found a recipe for Welsh cakes and made a batch to take to Bronwen's. I fixed my hair and makeup, and wore a green cashmere sweater with my jeans.

I liked Bronwen immediately; she welcomed me to her home, assured me that the Welsh cakes would be perfect for dessert since she had just opened a jar of brambleberry jam, and generally made me feel right at home.

"I made a couple of Gareth's favorites, tonight," she continued. "There are Glamorgan sausages, and Welsh rarebit. We try to eat meatless once a week here; I hope that's all right with you."

"I'm sure it will be lovely," I responded.

And, indeed it was. I asked Bronwen if she'd give me the recipes, and she agreed. I then helped clear the table while Gareth and Timothy played a game on the boy's iPad.

"You're the first woman in quite a while to whom Gareth has introduced me," she said.

"I've enjoyed getting to know him, and the work he does every weekend at Wisteria Cottage is a godsend. I'm afraid I don't know crabgrass from a chrysanthemum."

"Gary only went to Wisteria Cottage once a month before you arrived," she confided as we worked together in the kitchen. "It seems that I seldom hear of anything but Miss Rose from my son; my brother is a little more subtle."

I could feel the blush mounting in my cheeks. "I had no idea."

"Well, now you know … but maybe don't let on that I told you." She smiled. "Oh, and one more thing. I would love to have you join us on the class trip. I don't think Timothy would ever forgive me if I said no."

So it was that I joined Bronwen, a couple of mothers, and another teacher at the train station in Berwyn to take 40 excited Grade 2 students to London. On the train, I found myself repeatedly admonishing the children to stay with their field trip partner, not run, and so on.

I honestly wondered how the teachers did it, day in and day out, without losing their sanity. I would be relieved to have Gareth along, that was for sure.

Gareth waited on the train station platform, scanning the crowd for his sister and Rose. The two looked more than a little harried after they piled off the train, surrounded by a mass of children in their blue school jumpers.

"Uncle Gareth!" Timothy called, "We're over here."

As Gareth walked toward the group, Rose tucked an errant lock of hair behind her ear and heaved a sigh.

"I'm so glad to see you," she whispered as they hugged.

"Likewise." Then he turned his attention to the children. "I'm Miss Bronwen's brother, Gareth. I know you're all terribly excited; Timothy has told me you've been learning about dinosaurs. We're all eager to see them, but we need to be careful not to get lost. Each of us has a partner, yes? I need you all to line up, with your partner, so that we go two by two. If your mum is here, she's probably your partner. Miss Bronwen and Timothy will be at the front, and Miss

Rose and I will bring up the rear. Now then, everyone in line so that we can get on the Tube."

It had to be his experience as a teacher; there was something about Gareth that just made the children obey. Pretty soon, like ducks in a row, we were heading down the sidewalk, with the other mothers and their children, and the other teacher, interspersed in the crowd. We managed to stay together and get to the museum in one piece, at which point Bronwen and her colleague handed out worksheets.

"Everyone has their pencils, yes? Remember, you need to tick off which dinosaurs you see, and note a fact about them. That means reading the cards, not just running about. Have an adult help you with difficult words," Bronwen said. "And no running!"

Gareth took my hand in his; he looked particularly handsome in jeans, leather jacket, and a blue cashmere sweater. "You should see the sights too, Rosie. Let's have a look around."

Several times, he wrapped his arms around me and gave me another of his delicious kisses. He made me giddy as a school girl.

However, we were not as discreet as we might have hoped.

"Tim," one of the boys called out, "Your uncle is kissing Miss Rose! You'd better tell your mum on them!"

"Sometimes, when grown-ups like each other, they kiss," Timothy replied. "You do like Miss Rose, don't you, Uncle Gareth?"

"I do indeed. Now, let's see how far you are on that worksheet."

Gareth joined us on the train for the ride home; he'd stowed a weekender in a locker at the station.

"I hope you don't think I'm presumptuous," he said. "I'll get a ride share in the morning and take the train back into town."

My response was to settle down against his shoulder with a sigh and fall asleep. I didn't wake up again until we were in Berwyn. Parents were there to pick up their children and drive them back to Shalbourne, and we waited until everyone was on their way before piling into Bronwen's car.

"Are you staying with us tonight, Uncle Gareth?" Timothy asked.

"Not this time; I'm staying with Miss Rose at Wisteria Cottage."

"Oh." Timothy looked out the window; I could see his lower lip quivering.

"Saturday isn't far away," I said. "Maybe while your uncle works on the garden, you and I can work on your dinosaur report. I think my favorite was the ichthyosaur fossil found by Mary Anning. What about you?"

"I was going to pick the T. rex," Timothy said, "But everyone seemed to pick him because we got to see him walking around. Maybe I will pick the ick, um, fossil too. Will you help me?"

"Of course I will. And we will include some facts about Miss Anning, too; can you believe that people didn't think a woman was smart enough to find fossils? Isn't that silly?"

And thus order was restored before Gareth and I went into the cottage for the night.

After some discussion, we agreed that he should have a spot in the bathroom for his toothbrush and shaving things, and a drawer in the dresser for some clothes. It felt like an enormous step, having Gareth's belongings in the master bedroom with me rather than in the guest room for "just in case," but it also felt right.

When he joined me in the brass bed where I'd slept alone since my arrival, it felt more right than anything I'd ever known. I couldn't remember ever being so content.

After making love, I settled into Gareth's arms.

"Tell me about your life growing up," he said.

It was one of the hardest things I'd ever done. I told him about how I'd wanted to be like Aunt Susan. About how I was taught that being sensible and practical was the answer to everything. About how miserable I'd been for so many years. I even confessed how I'd hated every minute of business school when what I'd really wanted was to study literature and writing.

"I mean, I was good at it," I finished, tears coursing down my cheeks. "Really good at it. And I had what most people would call a successful career. But I was so unhappy."

After kissing my tears away, Gareth told me about growing up in Wales. About how work was hard to come by in Swansea and that he relied on his musical abilities to obtain scholarships so he could go away to school and not be another mouth to feed. About how he came to London for work, and how Bronwen moved to the Downs when Timothy had a chance to buy a pub called The Plough — a chance he was told about by Katherine Tremaine. About how Bronwen had sold the pub to another family when Timothy became too ill to work anymore. And a little bit about how he'd fallen in love a long time ago with the wrong woman and stopped cutting his hair after he broke off with her.

Then, he said something surprising.

"I feel kind of sorry for your mum, Rosie. Something must have made her very unhappy, to make her tell a small child that she shouldn't play dress-up or pretend. Every child should do that. Maybe you should ask her."

"Why?"

"Because people always do things for a reason, even if they don't clearly understand it at the time." He kissed my forehead. "At least you know why you did the things you did, even though they hurt."

We fell asleep in one another's arms; I was emotionally spent, but I felt safe and secure for the first time in decades. And I had something new to think about.

After Gareth went home the next day, I phoned my mother.

"I'm sorry to bother you so close to dinnertime," I began.

"It's fine, Rose. Your father is sleeping, so dinner is waiting."

"I want to ask you about something that happened when I was six …"

After I related the incident, I waited for my mother to deny it, or at least to say she didn't recall it happening. Instead, she surprised me.

"I remember it well, Rosie … and I wish with all my heart I could take it back." She sighed. "When Susie and I were growing up, everyone always talked about how pretty and vivacious she was.

How funny and charming she was. And me? I was always the smart girl. The nice girl who made good grades. But being the nice girl who makes good grades isn't nearly as much fun as being pretty and charming … and so I pretended that none of it mattered. Pretty soon, I had myself believing that being nice, polite, and smart, were the only things that mattered. And they do matter. But so does having fun, being spontaneous, and all of the things I stopped doing because I figured Susie had that all sewed up.

"And do you know what? I think all the time about the opportunities I let pass me by. Did you know I used to paint and draw? No, I don't suppose you did." A wry laugh. "But I stopped, because it wasn't practical to paint. Instead, you needed to work hard to get ahead in the world and not do frivolous things.

"Oh, Rosie. I was so envious of Susie. And when I saw you playing dress-up to look like her, I got angry. I was so upset that you didn't want to be like me … even though I didn't know who I was anymore. Can you forgive me?"

I could hear her choking back tears.

"Mommy, I forgive you. I didn't know."

"Of course you didn't, honey. And I didn't know how to tell you. But guess what? I am so proud of you. You took a leap of faith to go to England and write a book, and I'm sure it will be wonderful. I love you so much."

"I love you back."

We said our goodbyes and I hung up the phone. My cheeks were wet, and I didn't realize I'd been crying myself.

OCTOBER

Mis Hydref

It was, perhaps, inevitable that I would be felled by a migraine again. When Gareth and Timothy arrived that Saturday, I couldn't move from the couch; standing made the room spin and me nauseous. I managed to gasp out what was happening and where Gareth could find my injectable; Timothy sat down on the floor next to me.

"Miss Rose, are you going to be okay," he whispered.

"Yes, of course. I have medicine to help with this, but I haven't needed it in a long time."

"Only, my da had bad headaches before he died." His face was solemn and his lower lip trembled.

"Oh, Timothy. This is not the same. After your uncle helps me with the shot, I will be better in about fifteen minutes. I promise. Will you find a book on the shelf and read to me while we wait?"

Gareth had my injection in-hand, and I sent Timothy to the bookshelf while I bared a hip and told Gareth how to use the auto-pen. By the the time the boy came back to read me *Mrs. Tiggy-*

Winkle ("Because there's a hedgehog in the garden here"), I was covered back up.

Gareth did his gardening at what seemed like lightning speed; I was sitting upright and feeling a little better by the time he came back inside. Timothy returned the book to its shelf and I stood up.

"I'll fix us something to eat." I took a tentative step toward the kitchen.

"No, Rosie. You take it easy. I called Bronwen while I was outside. She's bringing lunch, and taking Timothy home."

"You didn't have to …" I felt dizzy and sat back down. "Maybe you did."

Bronwen knocked on the door and let herself in just a couple of minutes later.

"I'm afraid it's nothing fancy," she said, putting a bag on the game table. "But I sympathize; I used to get migraines, too. Come on, Timothy; we need to let your uncle take care of our Rosie."

"But I want to help take care of our Rosie, too!"

"I know you do, but just now she needs quiet. Uncle Gareth can ring us up later to say how Rose is doing, and if she's up to it we can all go out to The Plough for supper."

It wasn't lost on me that I had graduated to "our Rosie" somewhere along the way, or that I was invited to the pub that had once been belonged to the family. I thanked Bronwen, hugged Timothy goodbye, and then Gareth and I were alone.

He unpacked a couple of cans of Coke, some crackers, and a couple of meat and cheese sandwiches.

"I'll put the kettle on tea. Shall I put one of the fizzy drinks away for later?"

I nodded, and he handed me one of the Cokes and the crackers.

"My sister's telling the truth; she got them something awful when she was in high school. I remember her using fizzy drinks and biscuits to settle her stomach before eating something with protein. Happened about the same time every month …"

The look Gareth gave me told me that he knew exactly what had triggered the migraine.

I put my drink on the side table. "You don't have to do this, you know."

"I do know, and I don't mind. Being in a relationship with someone means taking the bad days along with the good ones."

"Are we? In a relationship?"

"I don't know what else you'd call it, *cariad* …"

Cariad. One of the few Welsh words I knew: love.

"It's just that I'll be going …"

"Yes. And we'll worry about that when the time comes."

My head hurt too much to argue. Still, I couldn't help remembering one of Aunt Susan's other sayings: people come into your life for a reason, a season, or a lifetime. It was impossible to tell which it was until after the fact.

Gareth pulled a featherbed out of the closet and retrieved a pillow from the bed upstairs.

"You stay here; I'll finish up the work outside and change clothes. Then we'll see about these sandwiches. And maybe a hot water bottle or heating pad for you?"

He tucked the warm duvet around me, made sure the pillow was in a comfortable position, and went outside.

I didn't realize I'd fallen asleep until he came back in and had changed out of gardening attire.

Gareth watched Rose as she slept. He was reluctant to disturb her; he knew how much migraines and cramps had taken out of his sister. He sat down in the chintz chair near the fireplace after moving Marmalade to the ottoman.

He thought about what Mrs. Tremaine had told him about Rose, and how surprised he was to discover a pretty girl feeling her way in an unfamiliar world, figuring out who she was and where she belonged, rather than an angry spinster.

We're very much alike in that regard. We just hide it in different ways.

The revelation surprised Gareth; if anyone had asked, he would have claimed there was nothing for him to hide. However, he'd been hiding from the world, despite still doing his work, by keeping that world at arm's length with his appearance.

Didn't you tell Rosie that people do things for a reason? That includes you, Gareth.

He absently undid the long braid and combed his fingers through his hair. By now, he knew how much Rose liked it down.

Gareth sat across the room from me, wearing jeans and a maroon henley. His hair hung loose over his shoulders. I lay still for a few moments, just looking at him.

How did this happen? I never could have predicted I'd find someone like him.

Maybe because I was so busy looking for polish and perfection instead of kindness ...

I sat up and stretched. "I wonder if I might have that other fizzy drink and a sandwich? And I think there's a hot water bottle under the bathroom sink."

"I'll get them; you stay there."

I couldn't imagine any other man I'd been with saying those words. Those polished, perfect men had expected me to wait on them hand and foot: to be the successful businesswoman and the perfect corporate hostess all at once. As for giving me an injection, I might as well have wished to receive a real, live unicorn for Christmas.

How had I wound up with such selfish men? Was it, like those starchy, no-iron blouses, just one more way of protecting myself? If they didn't want to bother getting close, I could protect myself that much more readily.

This trip was showing me things about myself that I'd never expected and, honestly, wasn't sure I liked. Thankfully, I could move forward.

In a relationship with a beautiful, kind man who brought me a sandwich, and tucked a towel-wrapped hot water bottle in across my tummy to help with cramps.

NOVEMBER

Mis Tachwedd

It took a while for me to realize that I was stressing over having no set schedule. With no office hours to keep, and the book out in the world, I was free to do as I pleased. I often took the train into London to visit the museums, or see a play with Gareth, and spent the night in the townhouse … where I, too, now had things in the bathroom and a drawer in the dresser.

I'd also taken over the kitchen more than once, making some of my favorite dishes for Gareth. He was particularly fond of my meatball and Italian sausage lasagne, a recipe I'd been given by a friend. I made enough so that there were leftovers during the week when I was away, and I preened under the compliments about my cooking.

It also took a while for me to realize that I liked my quiet life in England's Downs. I always told people I was a city girl, and I loved everything about London. But coming home to Wisteria Cottage was like greeting an old friend. I deliberately put thoughts of leaving out of my head any time they arose.

Then came the day I had hoped for but hardly dared believe might come: the agent who had accepted my manuscript had sold it to a publisher. I had an advance against future royalties and a request for another book. I would soon have enough money in my bank account to live comfortably in a hotel once I went home, so that I could take my time finding a new apartment and getting started on the new story.

I sent an excited e-mail to Aunt Susan, and then I called Gareth. It took me a few minutes to calm down enough to get the story out.

“I am so proud of you, Rosie,” he said. I could hear the smile on his face. “This calls for a celebration.”

“I’ll make dinner,” I said.

“No, Rosie. I’ll make reservations.”

Gareth hung up the phone.

“She did it!” He laughed aloud, the joy ringing through the room even though only Bella and Meezie were there to hear it.

He couldn’t remember the last time he’d felt so good. His Rosie was now a professional author!

My Rosie? What’s happening to you, Gareth? Do you dare name this feeling, even to yourself?

As I told my aunt shortly after I met Gareth, I'd never liked long hair on men. But when he picked me up at the train station, his mane caught up in a silver clasp at the nape of his neck, I realized I'd changed my mind. The wild waves contrasted with the beautifully cut suit he wore.

"There's a table waiting for us at the Savoy," he said as he took my weekender and carried it to the parked Rover.

I looked down at my jeans. "I'm not dressed for the Savoy."

"We have time for you to change back at the house, if that's what you're worried about."

"I didn't bring anything dressy."

"Then we'd best get to a shop."

In what was possibly the world's fastest run through a Marks & Spencer occasion-wear department, I found the perfect dress and shoes to match. I deliberately skipped over the sensible black or navy dresses. I didn't want to be that person any more. The mauve satin midi I chose, with its v-neck and three-quarter sleeves, was pronounced "perfect" when I came out of the fitting room to show Gareth. High-heeled camel pumps and blue bead jewelry completed the ensemble.

I changed back at the townhouse, pulled my hair up into a French twist, and fixed my face.

The Savoy? To celebrate my romance novel contract? There is definitely more to this man than initially met the eye.

We shared a delicious meal, and went back to the townhouse. We shared the bath and the bed, and held each other as we slept. I didn't want it to end.

But, of course, the real world reared its head soon enough.

I had an e-mail from Katherine Tremaine waiting for me that evening; she'd be coming home the day after Christmas. Of course, I was welcome to stay on at the cottage if I wanted to, and use the guest room for the remainder of my visit. Part of me wanted to go back home right away, but didn't want to miss Christmas in the region I'd come to love. It was only a month away.

I summoned up my courage and left a voicemail asking whether Gareth could pick me up at the train in London on Boxing Day since Mrs. Tremaine was returning, and whether he could help me find a hotel on such short notice. I said it was all right to call late, which he did.

"I'm conducting the village orchestra for the Boxing Day fête," he said. "I'll take you home with me afterwards; you're welcome to stay. I won't be around much, what with rehearsals for New Year's Eve, but there's plenty to do and see."

"Come for Christmas," I responded.

"I'm meant to go to Bronwen's, but I'm sure she'd love it if you came."

"I would be delighted. You can stay with me after."

"I can think of nothing I'd like more."

And now I had to do some shopping.

DECEMBER
Mis Rhagfyr

I sat outside the bandstand, clad in my purple puffer coat, mittened hands holding a cup of hot cider. Flash's leash was twined around my booted ankle, since his little master was waiting to perform in the village's Boxing Day concert. I sat next to Bronwen; the two of us were becoming fast friends.

Gareth raised his baton with a gloved hand, and the little village orchestra lifted their instruments and started the song they'd rehearsed for the past several days. Gareth's breath could be seen on the chill air. His long braid hung down over his navy cashmere coat; the red scarf I'd given him for Christmas was wrapped around his neck.

The second piece featured a woman singing in a language I couldn't identify; it didn't really matter, because it was lovely. Gareth told me later it was a Finnish winter song.

The final piece was clearly Timothy's shining moment; he clambered up the steps with his clapper and followed his uncle's direction perfectly.

After the song, Timothy came over to claim Flash. “Uncle Gareth promised if I did a good job today, I could play the clapper in the show in London next week for New Year’s. You will come, won’t you?”

“You know I’m going home just a little bit after that, yes?”

“I know, but you could still come, couldn’t you? Mum says I’m to wear a suit.”

“I am sure you’ll be very handsome. Of course I’ll be there.”

“I’m going to ask Miss Rose if she’ll be my forever lady,” Timothy confided to Gareth while Rose was upstairs packing her things.

“Is that so? Why?”

“Well, she’s nice to Flash, and she’d never leave Marmalade or Meezie out in the snow. Plus, she’s aces at my Count 10 game, and she taught me how to play Snap and Go Fish. She’s pretty, and she likes you and Mum. Mum says it's important that your forever person likes your family. Plus, she said yes when I invited her to the New Year’s concert. So, those are all good reasons.”

“They are indeed. But she’s a good bit older than you.”

“I will just ask her to wait.” Timothy turned his attention to his iPad.

"Gary, you're in danger of a seven-year-old beating your time with Rose," Bronwen teased.

"She's going home soon, Bronny."

"Then you need to decide what you want."

Rose came downstairs with two suitcases in-hand and looked around. "I hate to leave this place."

She put food down for Marmalade and snuggled the cat one last time. Gareth picked up her bags to carry them to the car as she left the keys on the desk.

One of the hardest things I've ever done was to take that last look around Wisteria Cottage and lock the door behind me. My life had changed so much in the months I'd stayed there; I would be forever grateful to Aunt Susan and Mrs. Tremaine for the opportunity.

I was quiet in the car, though; I knew I would miss that little house, and I was doing some grieving. It seemed that everyone else understood. Eventually, though, the silence was broken … and I felt my world fall apart just a little.

"How are the rehearsals going?" Bronwen asked as we drove towards her house.

"Better than I expected. Megan sounds marvelous." I could hear the smile in his voice.

In the back seat, Timothy and I exchanged a look. My stomach contracted and I felt a little ill. Surely I had no reason to feel jealous?

"I didn't know she was on the program," Bronwen said, looking out the window.

"Yes, she's been hired to sing for New Year's Eve. Working with her has been delightful."

"She's mean," Timothy piped up.

"Timothy!" Bronwen turned to face the back seat. "That's not a nice thing to say."

"People can change," Gareth replied, glancing up in the rear view mirror. "She's not the person she used to be. She was very unhappy before."

We dropped Bronwen, Timothy and Flash off and headed into London. This time, Gareth took my bags into the green bedroom.

"I think you'll be more comfortable with your own space; I'll be getting in late after rehearsals and wouldn't want to wake you. Plus, Bronwen and Timothy will be here over New Year's; I'm sure you understand." He was looking everywhere but at me.

"Gareth, is everything all right?"

"Fine," he said. "I just have a lot on my mind."

He hugged me and walked out of the room, leaving me alone with some rather catastrophic thoughts of my own. Perhaps I had a reason to be jealous after all.

I went down to the parlor, which was decorated with greenery over the fireplace and a Christmas tree in the corner. Bella and Meezie were asleep in front of the fireplace. I picked a book from the case that look interesting: a historical novel by Sharon E. Cathcart. I'd always wanted to check out her work

Gareth poked his head in to let me know that he had rehearsal, wasn't sure when he'd be back, and to not wait supper for him.

Well, a snack from the kitchen would certainly suffice for me; my stomach was in unexpected knots and I wasn't sure how much I'd be able to eat anyway. Hearing Megan's name on Gareth's lips had brought all of my insecurities to the fore

When he came in from rehearsal, Gareth tapped on my door. I was tucked into bed, reading the novel I'd picked out earlier.

He sat down on the bed next to me. "How's the book?"

"I'm enjoying it, but I could put it down with adequate inducement." I winked.

He leaned forward to kiss me while unbuttoning his shirt. "Will this do?"

Surely no man could kiss me like he did and be thinking of another woman.

I surrendered to his lovemaking, determined to focus on the moment. I nearly whispered “I love you,” but fear silenced me. Again.

New Year’s Eve Day

After making sure that Rose was ensconced in the guests’ bath, Gareth tapped on the door to the blue bedroom.

“Bronny, I need your help with something. I’ve been thinking about this for a while.”

Bronwen followed her brother downstairs and into his bedroom. He closed the door behind them, and then went into the bathroom for his shaving kit. He handed his sister the scissors.

“It’s time,” he said, and flipped his braid over one shoulder. “Keep Rose busy today. She can’t know. Not until tonight.”

A few minutes later, Gareth left the house, hoodie pulled up over his head, while Bronwen packaged the shorn braid in an envelope with donation paperwork for a children’s cancer charity and dropped it in the mail.

Bronwen insisted we should go get our hair done for the evening. "I made the appointment as soon as I knew you were staying," she said.

So, there we were in a salon that charged an insane sum of money … funds I had to remind myself I had … getting hair and makeup done for the evening. Every pin that held my hair in place would be worth it for Gareth's reaction; after a trim and adding some long layers, my hair was swept away from my face in a complicated arrangement of twists and ringlets. Upon learning the color of my dress, the makeup artist went to work with her brushes and shadows, making a sophisticated green and grey smokey eye. I bought a tube of the lipstick she used so that I'd have it in my purse for touch-ups.

We all looked quite elegant from the neck up when we went back go the townhouse; even Timothy had his hair cut.

Gareth was nowhere to be seen when we returned.

"Final rehearsals," Timothy said. "We never get to see him right before the show."

We changed into our evening wear; I had a green velvet dress with an asymmetrical design featuring one long sleeve and one strapless side, and some green and white rhinestone jewelry to go with it. The dress looked like it would be more at home on a fashion doll than a person, and I loved it. It was the least practical thing I'd ever owned.

"You look like a princess," Timothy said when I came downstairs.

"And you look like a prince, in that lovely grey suit and red tie."

We went down one more floor to the foyer to wait for the taxi that would take us to Gareth's show. I tried not to think about Megan and what her return might mean.

Bronwen told the cab driver where we needed to go, but I was busy making sure Timothy's seat belt was fastened. So, I was a little surprised when the car came to a stop and the driver opened my door.

"You didn't tell me he was conducting at the Barbican," I said as we got out of the taxi.

"Hmm, I was sure he'd mention it," Bronwen replied. "He's been doing it for years. My brother is one of the best-known maestros in London."

We'd had a gap in the weather, and the streets were dry, which meant I didn't have to worry about the hem of my dress getting wet. I hoped that Gareth would like it when we met up after the program.

"He said he was a music teacher who occasionally conducted."

"Yes, but he teaches at the Royal College of Music." She looked at me shrewdly. "You really had no idea?"

“Not a clue.”

“I suspect he didn’t want to come over boastful.” She paused. “He likes you, you know.”

“And I like him, too.” What an understatement that was; I’d admitted to myself, but no one else, exactly how I felt about the handsome Welshman. After all, I was leaving. Maybe I’d tell Aunt Susan that we’d both been right … or maybe I’d remain silent on the matter.

My ticket was at Will Call; Bronwen and Timothy had gone backstage since the boy was in the program. I had an aisle seat close to the front of the theatre, where an usher directed me and handed me a program.

I spent a few minutes people-watching, reading my program (noting the name of soloist Megan Gruffydd, as well as Gareth’s lengthy list of accomplishments and accreditations — how had he been so closed-mouthed about this?) and then the lights came down. The orchestra assembled, and then a spotlight came on, aiming toward the wings.

I felt a total fool when Gareth walked out in front of the orchestra and stepped into that light. His white tie and tails were immaculate. So was his fresh haircut.

The one that he hadn't had this morning when he'd rolled out of the bed we'd shared, kissed me, and told me to enjoy the day with his sister.

The one he'd vowed to only get when he had a forever lady.

As I'd suggested he do when the time came, his hair was close-cropped at the back and sides but longer at the top, where it lay in soft curls just as I'd imagined it would. In short, he was polished and perfect. Just the kind of man I'd always dreamed of having as my partner. I wanted nothing so much as to run my fingers through those raven waves.

But Megan had returned, and I was leaving. I had no right.

Gareth raised his baton, just as he had at the village fête a few weeks before, and led the orchestra through the program. Timothy, very proud in his little suit, snapped the clapper to make the whip sounds in the holiday piece.

I tried not to cry as I watched Gareth masterfully lead the orchestra with the same confidence that he'd employed on my borrowed garden and cottage. He was a man of many talents, to be sure, and one with whom I had foolishly fallen in love.

The third piece featured Megan singing; she was a beautiful blonde woman, and her voice was amazing. Gareth held her hand she made her curtseys. He then bowed over that same hand and kissed it before returning to the conductor's podium.

After the fourth piece in the program, Gareth stepped up to a microphone.

"We have one more piece to share before midnight, but I need to do something beforehand. I need to honor someone very special to me. I never expected to meet a woman like her, to be honest. She's made me see myself in a different light. I have never asked this question of any other woman, and I hope she does not think it inappropriate to do so in front of so many witnesses."

I got up from my aisle seat and walked toward the exit and the coat check, so that I could get a cab back to the townhouse. I knew what he was going to do, and I couldn't stand to see it happen.

"Please, may I have a follow spot?"

Gareth had come down from the stage. When he called my name, I turned back to look at him standing next to my empty seat. Then, he was striding up the aisle toward me.

"Rosie, where are you going? Please wait."

You could have heard a pin drop in the theatre.

"I don't want to watch you propose to Megan," I whispered when he caught up to me.

"I'm not going to propose to her, *cariad*; Megan is happily married. You're the one I love." He dropped to one knee in front of me and caught both of my hands in his. "My Rosie, I know you have to go home for now. But I'm asking, will you come back and be my forever lady? If you say you'll marry me, it will be the best New Year's gift I could ask for."

"*Cariad* ..." I could barely get the word out.

"Please, my lovely Rose, will you be my wife?"

All I could do was nod as the tears spilled over and streamed down my face. Gareth led me back to my seat, wiped my tears away with his thumb, and kissed me gently. When he was back on stage, he said "I'm the happiest man alive; Rose said yes."

There was thunderous applause, and then Gareth directed the orchestra and chorale through "Auld Lang Syne." Afterward, he led the audience in a countdown to midnight and everyone took their bows.

After the program, Bronwen and Timothy took me backstage. Gareth picked me up in his arms and spun me around.

"How beautiful you are tonight," he said. "I love you, Rosie."

"And I love you, Gareth." I succumbed to temptation at last and twined my fingers in his hair.

"That feels so good. Please say you like it like this," he murmured in my ear. "If you don't, it'll take a long while to grow out again."

"One more thing," he said, pulling a small object from his inside jacket pocket. He handed me the carved wood spoon, with an elaborate handle and a heart-shaped bowl.

"This is pretty old school. I want you to pick out your own engagement ring, but I need to give you this. It's an old Welsh tradition, and means I want to set up housekeeping with you."

"It's beautiful, Gareth. And it will be my honor."

"I'm glad you like it; it's the one my grandfather made for my grandmother. I've had it put away for years, waiting for the right woman to come along. We can hang it in the kitchen when we get home."

JANUARY

Mis Ionawr

"I don't want to go," I whispered. We stood just outside the security area at Heathrow Airport. I had my carry-on luggage, and had checked only one bag. The remainder of the things I'd brought with me a lifetime ago were at Gareth's.

"I don't want you to, *cariad*, but the time will pass quickly. And when you come back, it'll be to stay." He pressed a kiss to my forehead.

"Well, there are all the fiancée and spouse visas to get …"

"My practical darling. We know what needs doing, and we'll do it. Now, you need to get through that line."

I ran my fingers through Gareth's hair. "I love you."

"We have to say goodbye for now, *cariad*, but never forget that you're my forever lady. I love you, too."

I know he watched until I couldn't see him anymore, because I looked back over my shoulder more times than I care to admit. The last time, I saw his leather-jacketed back as he headed for the car park.

I had told myself I wouldn't cry, but I was wrong.

JUNE

Mis Mehefin

Obtaining a fiancée visa was time-consuming and expensive. I was more grateful than ever for the book advance; I stayed with Aunt Susan while I managed all of the paperwork and either selling or donating things I would no longer need after the wedding. I shipped a few boxes to Gareth so that I wouldn't have so much to worry about bringing with me.

I also sent some time talking with my publisher about the forthcoming book's cover, and they agreed to the one change I'd asked.

Gareth and I talked on the phone or FaceTime regularly; I missed him terribly, and I hated that I wasn't there to help with the wedding plans, even though he assured me that Bronwen and his mother — oh, God, I wasn't going to meet his parents until the wedding — had everything under control.

Still, it felt like things were moving quickly and before I knew it I was on a plane with my wedding dress hanging in the first class cabin's coat closet and a book cover proof in my suitcase to show everyone.

Gareth, Bronwen and Timothy were all waiting for me at Heathrow after I came through customs with my bags. Timothy held a sign that read "Welcome home, our Rosie!" That started the tears flowing. Gareth's kisses were the best greeting I could have asked for.

Once we were at the house, I took out the cover flat to show everyone. It showed a silhouetted couple on the porch of a wisteria-draped brick house

"Love in Bloom, Rose Llewellyn," Timothy read. "But you aren't Rose Llewellyn yet."

"I will be by the time the book comes out, though."

"And look," Timothy continued. "That's Wisteria Cottage, almost exactly. Is this book about us?"

"No, but it's because of all of you."

"I am so proud of you, my Rose," Gareth wrapped his arms around me. "I love you."

I doubted I'd ever tire of hearing him say those words.

AUGUST

Mis Awst

Time flew, and it seemed I'd barely unpacked my bags when our wedding day arrived. The furniture had been pushed back to the walls in the formal parlor, and the rugs rolled up on special holders I'd never noticed. A white runner bisected the room and two sets of rented chairs covered the floor on either side.

Bronwen had been as good as her word; she and her mother made all the arrangements, with the colors Gareth and I had chosen for flowers and decorations. The gentleman from the registrar's office would come to perform the ceremony, we would sign his book, and we would formally begin our life together.

If I could ever get past my nerves. Aunt Susan, Bronwen and I were in the green bedroom, where I'd stashed the dress I'd brought from America. Gareth had kept his promise not to snoop, and I hoped he'd like it when he finally saw me.

Aunt Susan was walking me up aisle. My parents had sent their blessings, but were unable to make the trip. My father's health was poor and he didn't feel up traveling. He had met Gareth via Zoom, where he was formally asked for my hand.

"Rosie, get your glad rags on," Aunt Susan said. "You don't want to keep that lovely man waiting."

She and Bronwen helped me into the ivory, cocktail length Chantilly lace gown, smoothing it over the crinoline that made it stand out from my knees. The modest ballet neck and three-quarter sleeves made it look like something from the 1950s. I had fallen in love with it immediately and, since we were having an afternoon wedding at home, it was perfect

I picked up my bouquet, a mix of flowers and myrtle leaves; the trembling from my hands transferred to the blossoms.

And then it was down the first flight of stairs, then the second … and finally to the parlor, where a signal from Bronwen to the quartet of Gareth's musical friends began the processional.

Timothy led the way, with two engraved wedding bands carefully balanced on a pillow. Bronwen told me he'd practiced at home just about every night so that it would be perfect.

I don't remember a lot about the ceremony; I had eyes only for Gareth, who waited for me at the end of the runner in a dark suit and tie. We repeated our vows and put the rings, with "Cariad" on the inside, on each other's fingers. The musicians played while we completed the registry and received our marriage certificate.

And then we were walking back down the aisle together, hand in hand. Husband and wife. I really was Rose Llewellyn.

The receiving line passed in a blur as well. I admit, I didn't initially notice that Bronwen couldn't find Timothy after the ceremony; he'd done his part, carefully carrying the Welsh gold rings that Gareth and I now wore, and then disappeared.

"I told him to stay with me," she said. "I'm trying to get the food out for the guests, and I can't scour the house."

"There's only so much house to scour," I said. "I don't know why he'd hide, but I want him in the photographs. Let me look."

I found Timothy sitting on the steps between the second and third floors, holding a purring Meezie on his lap. His lower lip trembled and his cheeks were damp.

I remembered many times in my own childhood when I'd hidden with a beloved pet and my heart went out to him. Flash and Bella having been put out in the garden until the guests were gone, Meezie was his best refuge.

"There you are! You did a very good job in the wedding, and you look so handsome in that new suit. What's wrong? Are you keeping Meezie from feeling lonely?" I tucked my skirt round my knees and sat down on the step beside him.

"I was going to ask you to be my forever lady. I even told Uncle Gareth. And he beat me to it. It's not fair."

I put my arm around his shoulders. "Well, I'm your auntie now. And aunties are a different kind of forever lady. My aunt Susan is friends with Mrs. Tremaine and your granny; she's the reason I came to Wisteria Cottage in the first place. Aunties are like best friends and fairy godmothers all rolled into one."

He looked up at me. "I hadn't thought about that."

"I feel pretty lucky today, Timothy. I got two forever gentlemen at once. Now, let's go have some cake and our pictures taken." I stood up and offered him my hand. Gareth was waiting at the foot of the stairs and we all went down together.

AUTHOR'S NOTE

This novella was born because of two different puzzle games. In one, I designed an English country cottage; in the other, I designed a London townhouse. As I finished my designs, I started wondering what kind of people lived in these places. I had made each of them cozy, special, and pet-friendly, so of course the people who lived in my homes had to love animals.

I admit, I didn't plan to write the story, but it nagged at me. I had begun studying the Welsh language for fun during the pandemic, and so I wanted one of my characters to be Welsh. Soon, Rose and Gareth's story was taking form.

What I didn't expect was how much it meant to me to finish this novella. Like many, I struggled during the pandemic. The words would not come, no matter how hard I tried; I was only about halfway through my work in progress after two years. But here came Rose and Gareth, in a short story originally intended solely for my own entertainment. And honestly, I came to love them and their story.

A note about some of the terms in the book is in order. The month names are written in English and in Welsh. Glamorgan sausages are a traditional vegetarian Welsh dish made with leeks, cheese, and breadcrumbs. Welsh cakes are a griddled bread similar to scones. Welsh rarebit is a heavy cheese sauce poured over toast. Recipes for all of these items may be found at any number of cookery sites on-line.

And yes, popty-ping really is Welsh for microwave.

www.ingramcontent.com/pod-product-compliance
Ingram Content Group UK Ltd.
Pitfield, Milton Keynes, MK11 3LW, UK
UKHW041850190726
13854UKWH00002B/809

9 798215 723302